COME TO THE DOCTOR, HARRY

STORY AND PICTURES BY

Mary Chalmers

Harper & Row, Publishers

COME TO THE DOCTOR, HARRY
Copyright © 1981 by Mary Chalmers
Printed in the U.S.A. All rights reserved.
First Edition

Library of Congress Cataloging in Publication Data
Chalmers, Mary, 1927–
Come to the doctor, Harry.

SUMMARY: Harry Kitten learns that a trip to the doctor
is nothing to fear.
[1. Medical care—Fiction.   2. Animals—Fiction]
I. Title.
PZ7.C354Cq   [E]   80-7910
ISBN 0-06-021178-4
ISBN 0-06-021179-2 (lib. bdg.)

COME TO THE DOCTOR, HARRY

One day Harry caught his tail
in Mrs. Kelly's screen door.

5

Mrs. Kelly was sorry.
She gave Harry a kiss and told him
to run home to his mother,

which he did.

"Well," his mother said,
"we had better go
and see the doctor."

"I don't like doctors," said Harry.
"Why, dear?" asked his mother.
"Because," said Harry.

"That is not a good answer,"
his mother said.

"Let's go now!"

The doctor's waiting room
was full of patients.

12

They found an empty chair
between a small dog and a big dog.

The small dog had a Band-Aid
on his ear. He told Harry
about the cat next door.

The big dog had a cast on his leg.
He told Harry about the doctor
who had fixed his leg.

There was also a lady with a rooster
who had a sore throat,

a boy with a frog in a box,

and a man with a cat on his lap
and a cat carrier beside him.

Harry hoped there would be
a kitten inside, but there wasn't.

"Now, come along," said his mother.
"You must sit quietly
and not bother anybody."

"Well, can I sit with him?"
asked Harry.

21

"All right," said Harry's mother.

Finally, it was Harry's turn
to see the doctor.

The doctor put some powder
and a bandage on Harry's tail.
"This tail will be fine tomorrow,"
he told Mrs. Cat.

And to Harry he said, "Shake?"
"Shake," said Harry.
"Thank you and good-bye,"
said Harry's mother.
"Good-bye," said the doctor.

As Harry and his mother were leaving,
in came three baby kittens.

"Don't be afraid," Harry told them.
"I just saw the doctor
and there's nothing to it!
See the beautiful bandage
he gave me?"

On the way home
Harry showed his tail
to everyone he met.

He told them how brave he had been,

and how his tail

would be fine

tomorrow.